It was breakfast-time in Greendale. Sara was bustling about and Pat was saying, "Just time for one more cup of tea!"

Julian was going off to school. It was time for Pat to be off as well, but where *had* he put his hat?

"Ah! That's where it is." It was under his paper.

"Come on, Jess," said Pat, "time we were off."

Sam Waldron was out early, too. "Morning, Pat! Where's your van?"

"Can't stop," said Pat, "I'm taking the bus . . ."

"Taking the bus?" said Sam. "What *is* Pat on about . . .?"

When Pat called at the post-office for the letters, Mrs. Goggins had a bright new bunch of keys jingling in her hand.

"Morning, Mrs. Goggins!" said Pat. "I see you've got the keys. Isn't this exciting!"

"Ooh, yes," said Mrs. Goggins, "and a fine morning for it, too."

"I'll pop back for the letters when I've got her warmed up," said Pat.

But when Pat came back, it wasn't his little red van that came buzzing round the corner. It was a brand new postbus.

"Well, Pat, you've got more than letters to deliver, today," said Mrs. Goggins.

"Don't I just know it," said Pat. "Granny Dryden wants a ride into Ingledale, to do her shopping . . ."

"And you'd best see if the Reverend wants a lift," said Mrs. Goggins. "His old car broke down on Wednesday."

"I'll not forget. Cheerio!"

"Bye, Pat!"

But, when the postbus stopped outside the church, the Reverend didn't seem to be ready . . .

"Oh, Pat," said the Reverend. "I wanted to go into Ingledale in your lovely new postbus, today, but, oh dear. I've tied these three knots in my hankie, and I *know* they're to remind me about something, but, bless me, I cannot think what it is."

"Well, Reverend," said Pat, "are you coming on the postbus, or not? I'll have to be on my way, you know."

"Don't wait for me, Pat," said the Reverend. "I'll get the old bike out, if I remember what it was."

There were letters for Dr. Gilbertson.

"Hello, Pat," said Dr. Gilbertson. "Are you driving the new postbus today? I wonder if you could collect something from the chemist's for me?"

"It's a pleasure," said Pat. "Cheerio!"

All the seats were still empty in the little postbus.

"I hope I'm going to get some passengers today," said Pat. "I feel sure that Granny Dryden won't let us down."

Sure enough, there she was waiting for Pat, with her stick and her shopping-bag.

"Well, Pat, *this* is something new," said Granny Dryden, as she climbed aboard. "What a lovely way to go shopping."

Pat, and Jess, and Granny Dryden were on their way. But they hadn't gone far, when Granny Dryden shouted, "Oh, Pat! Stop! I've forgotten my hat!"

And Pat had to go all the way back again for Granny Dryden's hat.

Over the bridge and round the corner, and there was Miss
Hubbard waving at them, with bags and baskets all round her.

"I think we have another passenger," said Pat.

What a struggle and a rumption Pat had, getting Miss Hubbard
and all her bags and baskets into the postbus.

"She's worse than a sack full of parcels," said Pat to Jess.

And then there was Ted waiting for them outside his workshop. "I'll have a ride into Ingledale with you, Pat," said Ted. "I need a new gearbox for the Landrover."

Ted's feet got mixed up with Miss Hubbard's baskets.
"Oh, Ted, do look where you're putting your big feet!" said Miss Hubbard.
"Sorry, Miss Hubbard, I didn't see your old basket there."
They had a tug of war to get the basket off Ted's foot.

"Now, then, *pull*!" said Miss Hubbard. "You don't want to have to walk round Ingledale with a basket on your foot! And it *isn't* an old basket, Ted, though it looks it after being stuck on your foot!"

"It used to be a lot quieter," said Pat to Jess, "carrying just letters and parcels."

They went on their way at last. Over the hills and along bumpy country lanes.

"Slow down, Pat!" called Miss Hubbard. "You're making me all wobbly."

Pat had to slow down. There was Sam's van in front of them, blocking most of the lane. It was a tight squeeze to get past.

"Pat," said Miss Hubbard, "can we stop for a little refreshment? I'm sure Sam has something nice on his van."

Granny Dryden said, "A biscuit would be nice."

Pat popped along to empty the letter-box whilst they all got out to stretch their legs.

"You'll spend all your money before we get to Ingledale," said Pat. "And we really should be on our way. I have the letters to deliver as well as you, you know."

It took ages to get them all aboard again.

"That's one thing about letters," said Pat. "They never get out for a biscuit."

They were on their way, at last. But, when they came to the
bridge, there was P.C. Selby waving to Pat to stop, and putting
orange cones all across the road.

"Oh, dear!" said Pat. "What now?"

"Sorry, Pat," said P.C. Selby. "You can't go this way. The old
bridge isn't safe. It's all this rain . . . these floods are dreadful."

"Oh, dear, and we're running late as well . . ." said Pat.

"I know a short cut . . ." said Ted. ". . . just go straight down here
. . . next left . . . no it's right . . . er . . . no, as you were, Pat, left it is.
LEFT! Through that gate. Watch it, Pat, it's a tight fit! . . . Down
here, Pat . . . don't worry, you'll be all right . . ."

Soon, Ted had them going through a muddy field.

"It feels like a ploughed field!" said Miss Hubbard.

"It is," said Pat.

They went down a very steep hill, and came to a dead end. The track just stopped in a blackberry bush.

"I'm not sure of the way, now," said Ted. "It's a long time since I came this way. It looks all different."

"I knew it," said Miss Hubbard. "We're lost! You don't know which-way from t'other, young Ted."

"That's not fair," said Ted. "I've been this way dozens of times. It looks a bit different today, that's all."

There was only one way to go, and that was *backwards*! Pat drove backwards all the way over the hill until they came to a road. Then he said, "*I* know where we are! This is the road to Thompson Ground."

There were letters to deliver. And Alf wanted to see the new postbus.

"How are you, Dorothy?" said Miss Hubbard. "I'll just stretch my legs for a minute."

Granny Dryden had been having a sleep. She woke up now.

"Where are we?" she said. "Are we there? Where's the market?"

"No, we're not there," said Pat, "but we should be. We've been having a tour of the countryside. We're at Thompson Ground, now."

Ted was having a look at Alf's tractor.

"Ooooooooooooooooooooooohhhhhhhh!"
Who was that? Look out! It was the Reverend Timms whizzing
down the hill on his old bike, and he couldn't stop!
"Lord save us!" wailed the Reverend as he whizzed past.

He went straight into Alf's barn, and fell off in a soft pile of hay. How lucky! Then, when he came out on wobbly feet, he said, "Oh, but I remember now. *That's* what the knots were for. One to remember my sister's birthday. Two . . . to remember to post her present."

"And three . . .?" said Pat.

"To get new brakes for my bike!"

"A very good idea," said Pat. "I wonder what made you remember?"

"Why don't you go to town in the postbus," said Alf, "and I'll mend your bike for you. I'll bring it round to the vicarage tomorrow."

"Time we were on our way," said Pat. "Come along everybody!"

Pat got them all aboard at last, and they were on their way once again.

It was twelve o'clock when they got into Ingledale.

"I've *never* been so late," said Pat. "Everybody back here, please, at two o'clock. And don't be late!"

"We'll not be late," said Miss Hubbard.

But . . . when two o'clock came, Granny Dryden was missing.

"We can't go without her," said Pat.

"I'll go and look for her," said Miss Hubbard. "She'll be in the market getting her potatoes."

Then Granny Dryden came back, but there was no sign of Miss Hubbard.

"Oh, there you are! Have you seen Miss Hubbard, she's gone looking for you?"

"Looking for me?" said Granny Dryden. "I wasn't lost."

"No but . . . I'll tell you what," said Ted, "you sit in the bus, and I'll go and look for Miss Hubbard."

No sooner had Ted gone . . . than Miss Hubbard came back.

"I can't find Granny Dryden anywhere," she said, "I think we'll have to report her missing . . . Oh! There she is, in the bus. How did she get there?"

"Well, you see . . . oh, it's too mixed-up to explain . . ." said Pat.

"And where has Ted gone?" said Miss Hubbard.

"Looking for you."

"But I'm not lost," said Miss Hubbard.

"I know you're not lost," said Pat, "but . . . oh, dear what a muddle . . . never mind . . . we'll just have to wait, and I don't know *when* we're going to get back to Greendale, but I'm going to sit in the bus and read my paper . . ."

Ted came back at last, and they set off home again.

There were more letters to collect on the way.

There were letters and a parcel to take to George Lancaster at Intake Farm.

"This postbus is a great idea," said George. "Do you think I could take a dozen hens to market in it, tomorrow?"

"Indeed not," said Miss Hubbard. "Just think of the feathers! We'd all be sneezing for a week. Oh, but what lovely eggs. May I buy a dozen, please? I forgot to get any at the market."

It was time to be on their way.

Dorothy was waving from her gate. What was the matter?

"Oh, Pat," she said, "Mrs. Goggins has been on the phone. She's ever so worried. She's wondering where you've all got to. Thinks you've had an accident with the new postbus. Why not come in and give her a ring?"

So Pat drove in.

"You must all come in for a cup of tea and a cake," said Dorothy. "You're welcome. You must be parched after your trip."

Pat went to telephone the post-office.

"Hello, Mrs. Goggins," he said. "Yes . . . no, we haven't been to Blackpool, just Ingledale . . . all safe and sound . . ."

"What a time we've had," said Miss Hubbard. "It's a wonder Pat managed to get us all home again."

"Now don't you worry about your old bike, Reverend," said Alf.
"I've given it a good oiling and tightened up all the nuts. It's as good
as new. It just needs some new brake-pads and all will be fine. I'll pop
round with it tomorrow."

They all enjoyed their tea.

There was a saucer of milk for Jess.

But Pat was looking at his watch.

"Come on, everybody!" he said. "Time to be off!"

"Cheerio!"

It had been a long day.

"Here we are, Miss Hubbard! Your stop," said Pat, and Miss Hubbard tumbled out with all her baskets full of good things.

"Thank you, Pat. Goodbye!"

The next stop was Granny Dryden's cottage.
"Where's my hat?" said Granny Dryden.
Ted found it on her seat, all squashed.
"You've been sitting on it," said Ted.
"Oh, dear, I never even felt it," said Granny Dryden.

Then it was time for Ted
to get out.
"Bye, Ted!"

31

When they came to the church, the Reverend said, "Oh, Pat, I still have a knot in my hankie!"

"Now then, Reverend," said Pat. "Is it a new one, or just one you forgot to undo?"

"I've forgotten," said the Reverend.

"It's a good thing Jess hasn't got a hankie to tie knots in," said Pat. "I expect he'd bury it in the garden."

And he left the Reverend, still puzzling over his knots.

"Time for home!" said Pat. "I hope there's something nice for tea."

Look out for more Postman Pat and Jess adventures in
Postman Pat and the Toy Soldiers
Postman Pat and the Barometer
Postman Pat and the Tuba

Scholastic Children's Books,
Commonwealth House, 1-19 New Oxford Street,
London WC1A 1NU, UK
a division of Scholastic Ltd

London ~ New York ~ Toronto ~ Sydney ~ Auckland

First published by Scholastic Ltd, 1992

This edition published by Little Hippo, an imprint of Scholastic Ltd, 1998

Text copyright © John Cunliffe, 1992
Illustrations copyright © Scholastic Ltd & Woodland Animations Ltd, 1992

ISBN 0 590 19817 3

Printed by Proost. Belgium

Postman Pat

the Bus

Story by John Cunliffe
Pictures by Ray Mutimer
Based on the TV Special designed by Ivor Wood